# I Was There...

# TITANIC

While this book is based on real characters and actual historical events, some situations and people are fictional, created by the author.

Scholastic Children's Books
Euston House,
24 Eversholt Street
London, NW1 1DB, UK

A division of Scholastic Ltd
London ~ New York ~ Toronto ~ Sydney ~ Auckland
Mexico City ~ New Delhi ~ Hong Kong

First published in the UK by Scholastic Ltd, 2015

ISBN 978 1407 14886 1

Printed and bound by CPI Group (UK) Ltd, Croydon, CR0 4YY

1 3 5 7 9 10 8 6 4 2

# I Was There...

# TITANIC

## Margi McAllister

■SCHOLASTIC

# CHAPTER ONE

My little brother took one look at the *Titanic* and his face crumpled like a sheet of paper. He burst into tears. I wasn't surprised.

"It's too big!" he wailed.

"It's a 'she'," said Freddie. "All ships are 'she'." I was surprised that he could say anything. That ship was astonishing.

Everybody was talking about how big the *Titanic* was, but I didn't understand it until we stood on the quay and stared up at the height and width of her, deck above deck above deck with four steep black funnels like slanting chimneys. That ship must have been taller than three houses on top of each

other and as long as our high street.

I picked up our little Edwin, swung him on to my hip, and carried him along Southampton Dock, pointing things out to him to stop him crying. There was plenty going on to tell him about, like the grand people arriving in gleaming motor cars. Some of those ladies looked as if they'd stepped out of a picture with their big feathery hats and dainty little button boots. They had maids bustling about them, and heaps of cases ready to go on board. Those cases were so big you could have slept in them. How could they need it all?

There were four of us going together – Ma, my brother Freddie, who was six, little Edwin, and me, and I was ten. The boys were dark-haired imps with big brown eyes like we all have in our family. Between us we had one trunk and Ma's straw shopping bag. I heard that the ladies and gentlemen in first class took everything from tennis balls to cars. Some even had little dogs with them. How could a ship float with all that and all those people on board?

Edwin was getting heavy. He was nearly four, too big for me to heave about, but I was used to it. He was still our baby. I had two big brothers as well, but they'd already gone to America with my Pa. We were moving to Pennsylvania to open a shop there, so Pa and the boys had gone first to get everything ready for our new life in America. Yes, I'd cried about saying goodbye to my Gran and Granda, and my friends, but it was exciting. The night before I'd been too excited to sleep.

I put Edwin down and took a firm hold of his hand before he could run off. I was hanging on to my hat with the other hand, because it was breezy by the water, when I heard a woman with a loud voice behind us.

"Would you look at that ship!" she said. "It can't possibly float!"

"Madam," said a man's voice calmly, "let me assure you, she can't possibly sink. She is the safest vessel ever built." I turned to listen and, honestly, I couldn't help staring! His uniform was so smart, from his cap with gold braid to his gleaming black boots! His little brass buttons were perfectly lined up, and so were the gold bobbles on his shoulders. His beard was white and very neat and he looked as fine as the ship.

He was explaining about the way the *Titanic* was made. The big underwater part of the ship, the part that made it float, was divided into watertight rooms like huge boxes. If water got into one – which wasn't likely, because the ship was strongly built –

it couldn't get into the others.

"So you see, madam," he said, "you'll be safer on this ship than a baby in its mother's arms." Then he looked down at us. I gave Edwin a nudge, because he was staring with his mouth as wide as a tunnel.

"Good morning!" said the man. "My name is Captain Edward Smith, and I'm your captain on this voyage. May I know your names?"

"I'm Daisy Hooper, sir, and this is my little brother Edwin," I said, and pointed to Ma. "That's my Ma and my other brother near..." I didn't know the proper words for anything, so I said, "that end."

He smiled. "The stern," he said. "The back of a ship is the stern, and that's where your cabins will be. The front is the bow. I hope you have a splendid trip! When you're an old lady, Daisy, you'll tell your grandchildren that you sailed on the maiden voyage of the *Titanic*!"

He went away to meet some of the first-class people and I wriggled through the crowds back to Ma, who was talking to a man in a white jacket. I found out afterwards that he was a steward, so it was his job to look after passengers.

"We weren't supposed to be on this ship," Ma was explaining. "The other one couldn't sail because there's a shortage of coal."

"It's your lucky day!" he said. "A lot of ships had to cancel because of the coal shortage and we've room on *Titanic*. There's never been a ship like her, she's a goddess of the sea. Believe me, third class on *Titanic's* as good as second class anywhere else. Were you told to bring your own food? You won't need it here. A ticket for this ship is like full board in a hotel. All meals are provided in the dining room. Welcome aboard, ladies and young gentlemen!"

Freddie's face lit up. The food would be enough to make him happy. We followed the steward over the gangplank, with our Freddie pulling ahead on Ma's hand and me hanging onto little Edwin.

"What's that smell?" asked Freddie loudly, which didn't sound very polite, but I knew what he meant.

"Fresh paint," I said, "because everything's new."

There were handrails on the narrow stairways down to the third-class cabins but I didn't dare touch them, they looked so shiny. I was scared that the boys would put dirty fingermarks on the new white paint – but the further we got, the more people we met, milling and jostling through the corridors looking for their cabins. There were women with babies and small children by the hand and, even though they were struggling with their luggage, everyone seemed to be happy. The number of our cabin was on the tickets and Ma was watching the rows and rows of doors – C100, C101, C102 – until at last she called out, "Here we are – C112, that's us!

Oh, look, Daisy, it's got our names on it!"

All our names were on the door, and when we got in I couldn't speak! Honest, I couldn't! The boys jumped on the bunk beds and bounced.

"Stop that!" said Ma. "We mustn't break anything."

It was a plain, simple room but as clean as could be, and everything in it was so new it was like looking in a shop window. There were neat little bunk beds with curtains across and facing the door was a hand basin! A gleaming white one with two taps!

"Is that real?" gasped Freddie.

"No need to look at a wash basin as if you've never seen one before," said Ma, but she was checking the door and the tickets in case we'd been given the wrong cabin. Finally she sighed happily and smiled.

"Go on, Daisy," she said. "Have a go with

those taps."

I turned them and they worked. Freddie wanted to try, too.

"Is it seawater?" he asked. Ma tasted it.

"Proper tap water," she said, and gasped as steam rose from the basin. "And a hot tap!"

"What's that on the wall?" asked Freddie.

"Don't touch it!" said Ma, but it was too late. He'd already put down the switch on the wall, and a bright light filled the room, making it look even better.

"Electric light!" I said. We'd never had electric light at home, just gaslight and candles, and the only taps were in the kitchen and the back scullery.

"Well, this is good!" said Ma. "Daisy, when we get to New York I won't want to get off this ship!"

By midday I didn't know if she'd even get out of her bunk. It was a nice enough day and not a bit stormy, but the rocking of the ship in the water made her queasy before we even started moving. The boys wanted to go on deck so I had to go with them, and we joined the masses of third-class passengers climbing up to the fresh air.

There's something you need to know about the *Titanic*. Everybody talked about the first-class passengers, because they were so wealthy and some of them were famous, like John Jacob Astor, one of the richest men in America. Second class was very smart and expensive, too. But most of the passengers were like us, travelling third class. They sometimes called it 'steerage' because the cabins were down in the bottom of the boat near the engines. The ship was organized so that we didn't go near the posh passengers. Some of those lords and ladies and millionaires had paid more for their tickets than my Pa could earn in a year, and they hadn't paid all that money to share a deck with ordinary people like us. They didn't want us under their feet. Mind, when it came to my little brothers I didn't want them under my feet either, but

I didn't have a choice.

The deck was so crammed with people that we couldn't get near the rail, but a big man said, "Let the littl'uns through", and we got to the front. There was a great flapping of white handkerchiefs as everyone waved to friends and family on the dock below us. The boys waved even though there was nobody for us to wave to – we'd already said our goodbyes to everyone we loved and I didn't want to think about that in case I cried.

I held on tight to the backs of the boys' jackets and didn't look down in case I got dizzy. Then the clock struck twelve and the ship made a horrible noise, just like a cow!

It turned out it was only the noise that ships make when they move off, but at the time I nearly jumped out of my skin and I wasn't the only one. Then we were moving,

really moving out of the dock, we were on that great blue water on the biggest, smartest, shiniest ship that ever sailed, on our way to Pa and my big brothers and our new life in the American sunshine. I had to remember every detail to tell them when we got there. Dad and the boys hadn't been on a ship with taps and electric light, I was sure of that. I thought we were the luckiest people in the world.

Then somebody said, "When do they serve dinner, so?", but he said 'they' a bit like 'day' and I guessed he was Irish. Lots of steerage people were, though most of them came on board the next day when we stopped in Queenstown, in Ireland. The boys must have heard the word 'dinner', or I'd never have got them away from the rail.

With a brother in each hand I looked up at the first- and second-class decks high above us. Never mind dinner, I wanted to feast my eyes on those ladies with their gorgeous hats and beautiful long coats. A fair-haired boy who looked a bit older than me looked down and smiled, then the ship made that awful noise again and I jumped.

I found out later that we nearly hit another ship on the way out. I wish we had. It would have been better than what happened.

# CHAPTER TWO

Dinner for us steerage passengers was served at long dining tables and the food was wonderful. At dinner there was soup and fish and a hotpot and pudding, and Freddie ate so much I had to take him on deck to be sick over the side. That night I lay in my little bunk, too excited to sleep. Breakfast the next morning was as good as dinner, with porridge and kippers and even baked potatoes, as well as heaps of bread and marmalade. People talked in languages I'd never heard.

"Those women talk funny," said Edwin.

"Shh!" I said. "Mind your manners. It's French." But I didn't really know what language it was. There were people from all over the world, so I told the boys it was all French.

That first day I wanted to explore the ship then maybe curl up on my bunk with a book and the electric light on – but Ma was still queasy so I had to mind the boys. They went wild, running about like a couple of puppies. That place was all corridors and stairways, and as soon as I found one of the boys I lost the other. Edwin hadn't learned to read yet, and even if he had, words like 'private' or 'crew only' on a door would have made no difference to him. Freddie had just run up a stairway when Edwin went charging through one of those doors that we shouldn't use. A chugging noise that went on all the time in the background was suddenly a lot louder.

"Freddie, get down here!" I yelled. "Edwin! Edwin, you mustn't go in there!"

But he already was in there. We'd be in trouble now! My face grew red and I was wishing that Ma would turn up and sort it all out when I heard a man's voice. Thank goodness, it was a kind voice.

"Now, young sir," said the man, and I could hear that he was Irish, "I wonder who's looking for you, so?" And soon they were walking hand in hand towards me: our Edwin and a short, wiry man with dark hair going grey and kind blue eyes.

"Is it this little scamp you're looking for, madam?" he asked.

Madam! I was only ten! "I'm very sorry, sir," I said. "Edwin, you stay with me and say sorry to the gentleman."

Freddie had come downstairs. He didn't do it to be good, he just wanted to know what the noise was.

"'Tis the engines," said the man. "Would you like to see how they make the ship go?"

"Are you the captain?" asked Freddie. The man laughed.

"I wish I earned his money!" he said, and squatted down to talk to them. "Captain Smith has a little beard and a very smart uniform covered in gold braid and brass buttons. I'm a deckhand. That's like an odd job man. They call me Paddy."

I introduced us and explained about Ma being poorly. He took us along a gangway, up a little stair and into part of the ship that not even the posh passengers could visit. It smelled of coal and steam, like a railway station.

"I can hear something chugging," said Freddie, and Paddy opened the door.

Before we even stepped inside, the noise hit me. Think of a great whooshing and thumping like a train, but much louder. I thought Edwin would cry but he didn't because he was holding tightly to Paddy's hand. We stepped forward on to a gallery, like an iron balcony going all the way round the room, and there we were in the engine room – the huge, swooshing, gleaming, thumping heart of the *Titanic*.

Imagine a row of giants all standing with their legs apart and their arms across each other's shoulders. But these giants were enormous metal giants, with square legs

and huge round drums where their heads
should be and the men walking round them
looked as tiny as Freddie's toy soldiers. There
were galleries everywhere, and ladders. Paddy
squatted down beside the boys.

"Do you see?" he said. "That's what keeps
the ship pushing through the sea, all the
way to America."

"We mustn't stay here, boys," I said. "We'll be in the way."

I said that because I didn't want to stay. It was all too noisy and looking down made my stomach tighten. I took Freddie's hand but he refused to move, then a voice behind me called, "Hi, Paddy!"

"Good morning, Master Jimmy!" said Paddy with a broad smile, and I turned round to see a fair-haired boy, maybe a bit older than me.

"Did I see you yesterday?" he asked. He had a funny way of talking.

"Yes, I remember you!" I said, as it came back to me. "You were right up at the top!" And as soon as I'd said it, I realized what it meant. I'd just met a first-class passenger!

# CHAPTER THREE

"Shall we have a look at the boilers today, Master Jimmy?" asked Paddy brightly. "Sure, I can take you in there. This is Miss Daisy Hooper, she's off to America for the first time."

"James T Gifford, ma'am," he said in a very grown-up way, and added, "call me Jimmy. Where in the States are you headed?"

"Where are you moving to, Daisy?" asked Paddy. He must have understood that I didn't know what Jimmy meant. After a while I got used to the way Jimmy talked, but I'd never met an American before.

"Silverpenny!" said Edwin brightly.

"He means Pennsylvania," I said. "My Pa's built us a house by the sea." Pennsylvania! It sounded magical to me, like a name in a story. "Do you know what it's like there?"

"I've never been to Pennsylvania," he said. "I live in New York City. My father's Augustus Gifford the Third."

What was that supposed to mean? Who were the other two Augustus Giffords?

"Mine's John Hooper the grocer," I said. I didn't mean it to sound funny but it did and we both started laughing, and the boys joined in even though they didn't know what we were laughing about, and I knew we'd all be friends. Paddy told Freddie and Edwin about the engines, and I chatted to Jimmy.

"My father has a shop, too," he said. "It's in New York City. Have you heard of Gifford's?"

I hadn't, but I soon found out. Gifford's was famous. It was one of the biggest shops in New York, except they called the shops 'stores', and Gifford's sold almost everything. Jimmy's big brother Gus was old enough to work for the family business. He'd been to London for a business trip and a holiday, and Jimmy had gone with him to see London.

"Gus is supposed to be looking after me," he said, "but mostly he hangs around with his friends, so I can do what I like."

There was a little pause and I had a feeling that he was lonely, and wanted a friend his own age on the ship. I felt a bit sorry for him, even though that sounds strange, feeling sorry for somebody so rich he can go in first class. I tried to think of something to say, but all I could come up with was, "Do you like the *Titanic*?"

His eyes lit up. "Isn't it marvellous!" he said. "Have you seen the pool? Have you been in the gym?"

I didn't even know there was a pool or a gym. But Jimmy was in first class.

"We're in steerage," I said, because it sounded better than 'third class'. "We don't have those things."

"Wanna come and see first class?" he said eagerly. "You should see the grand staircase!" I started to explain that steerage passengers weren't allowed in those places, but Jimmy just shrugged.

"You'll be with me," he said. "It'll be fine." But then Freddie came running up to grab my hand and tell me something and Edwin ran after him, tripped up, and cried. Jimmy and the engine room men had sweets in their pockets and the boys were soon calmed down. To distract them the men showed us the ladders that the crew used to get from one part of the ship to another. They were long metal or wooden ladders, with the rungs so far apart that it was too much of a stretch for Edwin's arms to get up at all, so Paddy carried him on his back all the way up to the next deck. The boys liked the engine rooms more than I did. I was still thinking of all those things Jimmy had talked about – the pool, the gym, the grand staircase. That was what I wanted to see.

In the afternoon Ma was a lot better, so I didn't have to look after my brothers. This was my chance to explore the ship with Jimmy, if I could find him. I wandered through the steerage rooms where people were playing cards and some little girls had made a house under a table, and went up some little stairs onto the deck.

"Daisy!" shouted a voice. Jimmy was waving, leaning over the rail so far I was afraid he'd fall.

"Meet you down at the engine room!" he yelled. I ran all the way and got there before him. The moment he saw me he grabbed my hand and nearly dragged me up a stair. At the top, a steward stood on duty beside a notice that read 'First Class Passengers Only'.

"Good afternoon, Master Gifford," said the steward. He looked at me as if I shouldn't be there, but Jimmy said grandly, "This is my friend, Miss Daisy Hooper. Her father is opening a store in Pennsylvania. I believe he and my father will be working together very soon."

What nonsense! But the steward must have believed it, or else he didn't want to argue with a member of the Gifford family, because he let me through. Jimmy guided me into a lounge.

The first-class lounge was so big and so beautifully furnished that you could forget you were on a ship at all. There was brand new carpet and a painted ceiling, and the walls were all wood-panelled with arches and mirrors, and even stained glass windows like in a church! There were shiny leather chairs, and even pictures on the walls and mirrors. All this, on a boat! It was full of well-dressed gentlemen smoking and talking or playing cards, and the air was so thick with cigarette smoke it made my eyes sting.

Jimmy led the way to a corner where three young men sat round a table. One of them was blond and looked like Jimmy, only older, and he stood up when he saw us. He was tall with such a nice smile, and he looked like a prince in one of those story books! I thought of the little town I'd come from. If Gus Gifford had walked down our high street, all the girls would have fainted.

"This is my brother Gus," said Jimmy proudly, and I could see he thought the world of his brother. "He's Augustus Gifford the Fourth, but we call him Gus. Gus, this is my friend Daisy Hooper."

Gus shook my hand, and I blushed. He was such a smart gentleman, and there was I with my plain pinafore and boots!

"What are you thinking of, Jimmy, bringing a young lady into a smoke-filled room?" said Gus. He reached into his pocket and put some money into Jimmy's hand. "Run away somewhere and buy yourselves a present."

"Thanks, Gus!" exclaimed Jimmy. You'd think Gus had just given him the Crown Jewels. But I know what it's like being the oldest in your family and I could tell that Gus just wanted to be with his friends, not his little brother.

"Thank you, Mr Gifford," I said, knowing that I'd gone a bit pink, and we went out into the clean, fresh air again. There was a deck with pretty chairs and tables where the first-class passengers sat drinking their coffee. I liked that and I would have stayed there, but Jimmy said, "Barber's shop! It's this way!"

Barbers? I couldn't think why he wanted to go to the barber's shop, but I found out when I got there. There was a little stall selling souvenirs, even teddy bears and dolls! Some of those dolls were so lovely I could hardly take my eyes off them, but I didn't say anything to Jimmy. They probably cost far too much money, and anyway I already had a doll. I'd had her since I was little, and didn't need another one. We bought four ribbons like the ones the sailors wore on their hats, with '*RMS Titanic*' embroidered on them in gold – one for each of us and one each for the boys – then went on deck for a while and watched the sea. It's strange, seeing nothing but ocean wherever you look. I wish I could describe the smell of the sea, but it's hard to explain. If I say it smells green and blue, salty and fresh, you either know what I mean or you don't, but it's a good smell. Breathing in the sea air was like a cold drink on a hot day. I gazed upwards and saw the lifeboats with their covers on.

"There aren't very many lifeboats," I said. "I mean, there are, but not when you think how many people are on the *Titanic*."

As we looked up, Gus and his friends wandered past. Gus grinned.

"You don't need to trouble yourself about lifeboats, Miss Daisy," he said. His friends laughed and I felt a bit silly and embarrassed.

"There are some more that you can't see from here," said Jimmy.

"This is the *Titanic*!," said Gus. "The unsinkable! Why would you want lifeboats on an unsinkable ship?"

I suddenly shivered. Gus took off his jacket and draped it round my shoulders.

"Are you cold?" he said.

"Not really," I said, whispering because I felt so shy.

"Paddy says it gets cold at sea," said Jimmy. "The crew have been talking about that. They say it'll be real cold tomorrow."

But I wasn't cold, and I didn't know why I shivered. I just did.

# CHAPTER FOUR

The boys fell asleep that night clutching their new *Titanic* ribbons. The Irish people were having a party, and from my cabin we could hear bright, happy music played on fiddles. Everyone was welcome to join them but I was happy curled up on my bunk reading a book by the electric light. That was such a treat, I almost didn't want to get to America. In the morning we were off again, Jimmy and me, exploring. Oh, that glorious ship! I've never seen anything so splendid in all my life.

I loved the grand staircase best. It was wide with a brand new carpet, the wooden

banisters shone, and the carving was so beautiful it could have been the stair that Cinderella ran down. It really was like a staircase in a ballroom from a picture book. Ladies glided up and down it, beautifully dressed with jewels in their hair, but none of them looked as kind and sensible as Ma.

Jimmy told me who some of them were. I remember Mrs Astor because she had a kind face. She was only eighteen, married to

John Jacob Astor, and expecting a baby. John Jacob Astor was one of the richest men in the world, and a lot older than she was. Then there was the Countess of Rothes. A real Countess, and she was so beautiful! There was even a tiny baby on the ship, Milvania, and the ladies were so keen to cuddle her that the stewards made them take turns.

In the afternoon, they let us into the gymnasium. I'd never been in a proper gymnasium before and I didn't know what all the things were. There were machines with pulleys and handles which were something to do with lifting weights, and the seats with poles attached were rowing machines! Rowing machines, on a ship! Children weren't allowed on those. There were wall bars to climb but I couldn't climb those in case my underwear showed, so we didn't stay long. In the lounge there were stewards serving tea and a band playing dance music and popular songs. I'd never heard a band so good as that, and there was a surprise coming for me. Gus was there with his friends – mostly he chatted with them and flirted with the girls, but he ordered lemonade for us.

The man who led the band – I found out afterwards that his name was Mr Hartley – came over and said something to Gus. I saw them glance at me, and that bothered me. They must have realized that I was a steerage girl, and any minute now a steward would come and tell me to leave! I got up, ready to leave before they could throw me out, but then Gus said,

"Don't go, Daisy! They're just going to play for you!"

They began to play. They were looking at me, and I felt myself turn red. And do you know what they played? *Daisy, Daisy, give me your answer, do…*

Honestly, it made me feel like a princess, but at the same time I didn't know where to look. I was glad when they finished. But I loved it, too. As soon as they'd finished I got up to go because Gus's friends were still looking at me, and Jimmy said,

"Wanna come and see my stateroom?" What we called 'cabins' were supposed to be called 'staterooms'. We went along a carpeted corridor.

"But this is a sitting room!" I said when I got there. That's what it was — a very comfortable sitting room with armchairs, carpets, a table, and even a grate with an electric fire in it! The walls were wood-panelled, just like that beautiful lounge. There was a bed, too, with a quilt and the whitest of sheets.

"Do you share that with your brother?" I asked.

He laughed and opened a door. "This is Gus's room," he said. "It joins onto mine."

I peeped in. Gus had a lovely big room like this all to himself, too!

"You have all this space, just for you?" I said. I sat on the chair and bounced on the bed, imagining myself living in that room with a steward bringing me tea. I wouldn't want to go on deck! It made me laugh, but it made me wonder what it was like, too, to have a room like that.

"It gets lonely," said Jimmy, and for a moment he looked very sad. I guessed that he had to go to bed long before Gus did. Then he gave a little shrug and said, "Do you want to go in an elevator?"

I didn't know what an elevator was. I soon found out when we went back on deck.

The elevator was like a big cupboard that carried you up and down so you didn't have to use the stairs. There was a steward in there who shut two metal doors and I hoped Jimmy couldn't see how scared I was when those doors banged shut. I felt like a monkey in a cage. Then the steward pulled a handle and we just – sort of – sank! Then there was a little bump, he opened the doors, and we were back beside that beautiful staircase. I felt wobbly with amazement. We did elevators over and over again after that, because I wanted to prove that I wasn't scared any more. When it was time for me to go and have tea, Jimmy said, "See you tomorrow?"

"Where shall we go this time?" I asked.

"I haven't been to your part of the ship yet," said Jimmy hopefully.

I told him there was nothing much to see. Steerage was fine and I still loved our little cabin – I couldn't think of it as a stateroom! But what would Jimmy think of it?

In the morning I still wasn't in any hurry for Jimmy to see our cabin. We found Paddy, who showed us more stairs and ladders that were only for the crew. In the bow we saw the bunks where the crew slept. There was a post office, too. The *Titanic* wasn't just a ship for passengers, she was also a mail ship, carrying letters across the Atlantic. But Jimmy was still asking to see our cabin and I couldn't put it off forever, so at last I took him to see it.

I thought I'd never get him out of there. He stood looking at the little bunks and the washbasin, and finally said, "This is so good! You never told me it was like this! You lucky girl!"

I think he just loved it because it was so small and cosy. He lay on all the beds in turn and wanted to know who had the top ones. He closed and opened the curtains.

"It's like a little secret house!" he said with his eyes shining. "Right down in the bottom of the ship like rabbits in a warren! Are they all like this?"

They were as far as I knew. We were still there with Jimmy staring round as if he'd walked into a magic cave, when the door of the cabin opposite banged open and a small boy nearly crashed into me.

"Excuse!" he said cheerfully. He was dark-haired and bright-eyed, with a big smile. "Excuse, miss!" he said again. Behind him I could see a little girl in the room, sitting on the floor. She was so like him that I knew she must be his sister, and they talked to each other in a language I didn't understand.

Neither of them spoke much English, but with a lot of pointing and miming we managed to have some sort of conversation. It seemed that there were lots of empty staterooms. These two used this one as their own playroom, and they happily showed us where there were more empty rooms. They were fun, they never stopped smiling. We found an empty cabin and Jimmy sat on a top bunk, swinging his legs and telling me his idea.

# CHAPTER FIVE

Jimmy's plan was this – he wanted to spend a night in one of those empty cabins, all by himself. It would be like camping out, he said. An adventure. He'd go back to his own room first thing in the morning and nobody would know he'd been away.

"Gus looks in on me at night," he said. "Sometimes I'm sleepy and I don't open my eyes, but I hear him come in to check I'm all right. I guess if I put a pillow or some sort of bundle in the bed he won't notice that it isn't me. Hey, you could stay in my stateroom if you like!"

"I couldn't," I said. "Ma would miss me."

It was a lovely idea, though.

We went up to the first-class promenade deck where you could be inside in the warm, but still get a good view of the ocean from the window. Even there I was getting cold, and soon I went down to steerage for my coat.

"Cold?" asked Paddy. "You're in the North Atlantic now, my girl. We're making good time, so. You'll soon be in New York and seeing your daddy again."

I lay awake that night. Maybe it was because I knew that Jimmy had sneaked off to a steerage cabin for the night, or maybe it was just because I'd had an exciting day. Edwin was muttering in his sleep and I could hear the sounds of other passengers in the corridor. Finally I decided that there was no point in trying to sleep, so I put on the light and looked at Ma's watch. It was nearly eleven o'clock at night.

I'd spent so long running round that ship that I was pretty sure I could get up to first class without Jimmy, and his stateroom would be empty. It might be locked, but it was worth a try.

I put on my dressing gown and a pair of thick stockings, because it had been cold in the afternoon. Nobody stopped me going up to first class and I hurried to Jimmy's stateroom. It was unlocked!

First, I put on the lights and the electric fire. Then I curled up in an armchair by the fire and pretended to be a proper young lady with my own stateroom. But the fire made me yawn, tiredness crept up on me, and at last I climbed on to that big soft bed. I pulled the pillows round me, wrapped myself in the quilt, and thought myself the

luckiest girl in the world. I only meant to rest a bit, not to fall asleep.

A jolt suddenly woke me. At first I thought it was just a dream, like when you dream that you're falling, but then I heard a tearing sound like a piece of material being ripped far away. After that came silence. That was strange. I had become so used to the thrum of the engines that I didn't notice it any longer, but I noticed when it wasn't there. I sat up, wrapped in the quilt, and listened.

Cabin doors were opening. People were calling for stewards, asking what was happening.

"A small problem," said a steward. "We'll soon have it fixed and get going again." Then somebody said, "Iceberg? Really? An iceberg? Can we see an iceberg from here?"

I'd heard of icebergs, the mountains of ice rising up from the sea and lying deep and dark beneath it. I could hear everyone talking about it, and a lady was telling her maid to fetch her coat so she could go on deck and have a look. I wanted to see the iceberg, too, but suddenly there were a lot of people about and I didn't want to be in trouble for being in first class when Jimmy wasn't there to help me. I stayed quietly in a corner of the stateroom, and was still there when a steward came past knocking on the doors.

"Ladies and gentlemen!" he was calling, "Kindly put on your lifebelts!"

I opened the door, just a little. He was coming nearer, carrying a pile of what looked like flat white boxes, but I knew they were lifebelts for helping people to float in water. If the ship was unsinkable, why did we need those? Then Gus came pelting along the corridor and I turned hot and cold. I was sure to be in trouble now.

"Jimmy!" he was yelling. "Jimmy!"

He snatched a lifebelt from the steward then pushed his way into the cabin, not even seeing me. With a swish he pulled back Jimmy's bedclothes, then ran into his own room and back out into the corridor.

"What's happening?" he asked the steward urgently. "Have you seen my brother?"

"Excuse me," I said timidly, and at last he saw me.

"What are you doing there? Where's Jimmy?"

# CHAPTER SIX

"He's..." I began, but I couldn't get my words out. Too much was happening – I was in the wrong place, Jimmy was in the wrong place, people were coming out of their cabins and wanting to know what was happening, stewards were striding about with heaps of lifebelts, Gus was rattling out questions... Whatever was going on, there was no time to explain what I was doing there.

"He's this way," I said. I grabbed Gus's hand and dragged him past the cabin doors and the women in their silk dressing gowns. When I reached the stairs to steerage, he hesitated.

"This is the wrong way," he said.

"No it isn't," I said, and as we ran I told him about Jimmy spending the night in steerage.

"Why didn't he tell me?" muttered Gus. "Do you know where to find him?"

"I know sort of where," I said, but I didn't know exactly which stateroom Jimmy had gone to. Then I saw Paddy coming towards us, Paddy with his blue eyes and kind smile, and immediately felt happier. Nothing too bad could happen, I thought, when Paddy was there.

"I see you've got your lifebelts," he said. "Best to put them on, so."

The lifebelts fitted over our heads rather like bibs, and fastened at the sides. My hands were cold, so Paddy helped to tie mine.

"And now get yourself up on deck," he said. "And you too, sir."

"What's happening?" demanded Gus.

"I really don't know, sir, but they're having problems in the engine rooms," said Paddy. "So it's lifebelts all round. No need to panic, but I'd advise you to make your way to the deck."

"My brother's down here somewhere!" said Gus, and pushed past us to run along the corridor, knocking on doors and shouting Jimmy's name. The stewards were working their way through steerage with lifebelts now, just as they had in first class.

"No need to panic," said one of them. "Stay where you are, but put these on."

I grabbed an armful of lifebelts and ran to our cabin. Ma was getting out of her bunk and putting on her dressing gown.

"What are you...?" she began, but I didn't let her finish.

"We need to put these on," I said. Freddie was sitting up and rubbing his face, but Edwin just opened his eyes and shut them again.

"Something's wrong, isn't it?" she said. "I felt a jolt. Everything shuddered."

The jolt, the tearing sound. The stewards

with lifebelts. All those people getting excited because they'd seen an iceberg. A cold feeling ran down my back and arms as if I'd touched ice myself and I guessed what must have happened. We had hit the iceberg and it had ripped through the bottom of the ship. Whatever was going to happen next, I didn't want to be locked away down here. We needed to be on deck where we could see what was going on.

"We'd best get on deck, Ma, and it'll be freezing up there," I said.

"Boys, up you get and wrap up warm," said Ma. "Daisy, you'll need your hat."

She gave me my hat and lifted Freddie down from his bunk. While she helped him to get dressed I woke Edwin – poor little love, he was still warm and heavy with sleep and only wanted to go back to his bed. I got his lifebelt over his sweater and his coat over his lifebelt, but I couldn't fasten the buttons. I stuck his little toy rabbit in his coat pocket. He was still falling asleep on my shoulder so I tried to carry him, but with all those clothes on he was the size of a bear and much too heavy.

Somebody was in the doorway. I looked round and saw Jimmy in his pyjamas and dressing gown.

"I think the ship might..." he began, but I didn't let him finish.

"Shh!" I said, because I didn't want the boys to hear him say 'sink'. "Not with my little brothers on board, it isn't. Your Gus is looking all over for you."

"I went looking for him in first class," said Jimmy. "Couldn't find him anywhere. They're getting the covers off the lifeboats."

"Jimmy!" yelled Gus, pelting furiously round a corner. "What are you playing at? Where have you been?" He didn't wait for an answer, just pushed a lifebelt over Jimmy's head. "Fasten that and get on deck!"

"But there's all the others!" I said. "The Irish people, and..." I was thinking of the two children playing in the empty cabin, but I couldn't remember their names. Gus lifted Edwin out of my arms, said "Follow me!" and ran so we all ran after him, banging on doors and shouting to people to get on deck. Doors were opening, more people were joining us, tying on their lifebelts as they ran. Round the corner, we found a steward.

"No need to panic," he was saying. "Just wait in your cabins for instructions."

Some people did as he said, but not all of them. The corridors were filling with passengers now: Irish girls with shawls wrapped over their lifebelts, mothers with babies in their arms, and a dozen different languages were all being spoken at the same time. Everywhere was crammed. A steward was guiding women and children up the stairways, but just a few at a time. It was a wide stairway, but not wide enough for everyone trying to get up.

Jimmy and I had spent the whole journey exploring that ship. We knew all the ways around it.

"Stair to the second-class deck," said Jimmy, because that was the nearest. "Follow us!"

But when we got to the second-class stair we found another throng of frightened people, all women and children pressing forward. In front of them, two stewards blocked the way.

"They can't do that!" said Jimmy.

"Keep calm!" called one of the stewards. "Stay here, and stay calm!"

But they mustn't stay here, I thought. If the ship really was sinking, they needed to get to the lifeboats. Some were crying, some were praying, some were telling the children that everything would be all right. Above the murmurs of Irish women saying their Hail Marys, I heard something new. It was a creak, then another and another. Something seemed to knock against the side of the ship.

Jimmy and I looked at each other, knowing what that sound meant. On the unsinkable *Titanic* the lifeboats were being lowered, and we were trapped below the decks.

# CHAPTER SEVEN

Gus was tall. He stood on tiptoe.

"There are girls at the front," he said, and raised his voice to shout to the stewards. "Those young girls at the front need to get out! Let them through!"

"Let them through!" yelled Jimmy and I, and other people took up the cry. A man hurrying to the deck behind the stewards shouted it too – "Let the girls through!" – and it was such a commanding voice that, at last, the stewards gave way. The girls at the front ran for the deck and the others followed, but the stewards slowed them down. I suppose people might have been trampled if they'd all pressed forward at once, but how long would it take to get them all on deck?

"This is going to take too long," I said to Jimmy. "We'll try the crew ladder." We led the way back to the engine rooms. There were passengers running around like stray dogs, so we told them to follow us. It was easy for Jimmy – he was straight up that ladder – and I suppose Freddie wanted to show that he could climb as well as Jimmy so he skimmed up after him. I had to tuck my nightie into my knickers, and I don't know how Ma managed. Gus took off his jacket and made it into a kind of sling to tie Edwin to him so that he had both hands free.

Rung by rung we climbed up, away from the heart of the ship and up into the dark. From somewhere I could hear water and breaking glass. I was glad I had my thick stockings on, but even so the rungs felt colder and colder under my hands and feet as we worked our way up. My legs ached and the chill ran right through me. I could hear Freddie's boots on the rungs above me and Gus, with his American way of speaking, keeping our Edwin calm.

"It'll be just fine, little man," he was saying. "I've got you. It's just fine."

The air grew even colder. My feet cramped painfully. I felt that I'd been climbing this ladder all my life and always would be. Then there was light above me, and Jimmy gasped, "It's freezing! What's going on? What's that?"

I climbed out and pulled my dressing gown tight. The air was so bitter with cold that I could hardly breathe. A mountain of ice reared to one side of us like a monster. High up on the ship, cranes creaked, chains swayed, and lifeboats were lowered onto the deck. Stewards were trying to keep everyone calm, but I don't think they really knew what was happening either. Passengers in smart clothes and lifebelts scurried from one end of the deck to the other, looking for someone to help them. Women with white, strained faces held children tightly by the hand and watched the lifeboats the way a dog watches for food. Somewhere a small child was crying softly – I looked round to see one of the third-class women with her little boy in her arms, and beside them was Mrs Astor, one of the richest women in the world. She wore a fur shawl over her shoulders and I felt warmer just looking at it, but then she took it off, wrapped it round the little boy, and disappeared into the crowd.

In the middle of all this, there was music! The band was playing ragtime – the happy,

jaunty music that makes you want to jump up and dance across the floor. It sounded busy, if you know what I mean. It seemed to tell us to get up, get moving and get on with things, and even made me think that everything would be all right – except that it couldn't be.

"Women and children this way!" called one of the crew. "Women and children first!"

Gus handed Edwin into my arms and I wrapped my arms tightly round the bundle of my little brother. I pressed my frozen cheek again his warm little woollen cap, and heard Gus whispering to Ma.

"May I leave my brother with you, ma'am?" he asked.

Ma nodded, and put her hand on his arm for a second as if to reassure him. He bent down to speak to Jimmy.

"Stay with this lady and do as she tells you," he said. "See you soon!"

"Where are you going?" asked Jimmy.

"There are still people down there," he said. "Gotta get them up that ladder. See you later!"

He ran back along the deck and for a moment it looked as if Jimmy would follow him, but Ma put a hand on his shoulder. She took Edwin from me.

"This way," she said. "Quick sharp, now."

"I'm cold," said Freddie. "Ma, I left my bag in the cabin, can I go and..."

"No you can't," said Ma, and managed a brave smile. "We have to get off the ship, quickly. Be brave, it's an adventure."

Freddie looked as if he didn't want an adventure. His lower lip quivered and I pressed his hand to comfort him. He just looked like a little boy shivering in the cold and separated from the few possessions he had. He only wanted to be back in the warm cabin, with none of this happening. I understood that, because I felt the same.

Lifeboats dangled above the ship, jolting and jerking as they were lowered on either side. Against the great glorious *Titanic*, they looked like toys. More and more people gathered on the deck, so many for so few boats. I knew there weren't enough, and fear made my stomach clench.

A boat was already moving away, and I caught a glimpse of the Countess of Rothes taking an oar and helping to row. They were putting one or two crewmen in every boat to row and steer, but passengers had to help, too. I could row a bit, I could do that. The shout of "women and children first!" went up again.

We were near the front. I held Freddie's hand tightly. An officer was helping a woman with two little girls onto a boat. There was a young lad with them too, not much older than Jimmy, but I heard the officer say something about "no boys", and the mother begging him to let her son stay with her.

"They're not letting boys on, except little ones," said someone. "Older lads have to take their chance with the men."

"Go on, then," said the officer, and the boy stepped quickly into the boat. "But no more boys!"

I stood closer to Jimmy. There was a rush of cold to my head as Ma whisked my hat off and crammed it onto Jimmy's head.

"Stay close together," she whispered. "Jimmy, keep your head down. You're a girl."

I took one look back at the deck and it was like a nightmare where nothing makes sense. People ran about in their nightwear or evening clothes, there was shouting and pushing, weeping and praying and all the time the band played ragtime as if nothing was wrong, though the cold was so bitter I didn't know how they could still play their instruments. A bang made us all look up, and sparks showered from the air.

"Fireworks!" shouted Freddie in delight – only these rockets weren't fireworks, they were a signal to any other ships nearby to come and help us. As far as I could see there weren't any ships. There was just the dark, icy sea and the sky pierced with stars like needles.

I closed my eyes tightly and opened them again, hoping that it was all a bad dream and I'd wake up in my cabin. But it was real – the biting cold and terror, the noise – it was all real and I could forget everything I'd been told about the 'unsinkable' ship. The great gleaming *Titanic*, the goddess of the sea, was filling with water and dropping down to the ocean bed, and she would take us all with her unless we stepped into that wobbly lifeboat. There were some already on the water, looking as small and frail as paper boats on a pond. The Countess of Rothes rowed steadily.

All we had – our clothes and books, shoes, hairbrushes, my doll and my pencils – was in our cabin. My doll had been with me since I was tiny, and it seemed cruel to let her sink away. But I mustn't think about her. I had to be grown up about this and help Ma.

Two men helped Ma into a lifeboat, and swung the boys over to her, then reached out to me. Scared and shaking with cold, I climbed up onto the rail of the *Titanic* and into the little boat that swayed in the air so badly I had to hang on to the person nearest.

"You're all right, sweetheart," he said.

"Paddy!" I cried. "It's you!"

He gave me a quick, warm hug. "Sure, I won't leave you, Miss Daisy," he said. "Master Freddie, you come to Paddy, now!"

The trick with Jimmy's hat had worked and he was in the boat beside me, looking back up at the ship. More people were getting in, and with every step the boat rocked more.

"Let me through to the tiller so I can steer, so," said Paddy, stepping over and around people to the tiller so he could guide the boat when it was lowered. "Can any of you young ladies row?"

"I can!" said Ma, and so did a Scottish

woman and an American lady I'd seen in first class. They settled themselves onto the benches as more women got in, hugging whimpering children wrapped in shawls, and I'm afraid I curled up my fist tightly and bit into it because I couldn't believe that this little boat could take the weight. There was ice in the water below us – Freddie was watching me so I took my fist from my mouth and smiled to make him think there was nothing to worry about. But my toes, my stomach and my teeth were all clenched tight with fear.

"It's all right, Freddie," I said, and hoped he believed me. Around me, women were waving to their husbands on the deck and shouting messages, and I was so, so glad that my Pa and the boys were all safe in Pennsylvania. Slowly the boat was lowered until she touched the water and the ropes holding her were cut free. Afraid that we would go down and keep going down, that the icy water would lap around us, I squeezed my eyes shut.

"We're going to sink!" wailed someone.

"No we're not," said Ma sharply.

"Let's pretend it's just a wee row across the loch on an evening," advised the Scottish woman.

"Now, where's my little sweetheart?" called Paddy. "And Freddie, and you too Master Jimmy, you come and sit by me. Eddie, you too. That's all right, so."

Paddy sat at the tiller to steer and we huddled together for warmth on a bench near him. I wrapped my arms round Freddie and Edwin to keep them as warm as I could.

"Now let's get away," said Paddy. As we rowed away I could still hear ragtime music and the sounds of people crying. Jimmy still gazed back at the boat, scanning the crowd along the rail, and I knew he was watching for his brother.

I nearly said to him, "It'll be just fine," because that's what Gus had said to our Edwin. But I was afraid it wouldn't be.

# CHAPTER EIGHT

"Row, ladies!" said Paddy at the tiller. Somebody put a shawl round my shoulders, and I pulled it around me gratefully. I looked up to say thank you and saw the American lady from first class. She was looking past me at Jimmy.

"Aren't you the young Gifford boy?" she asked.

"Yes, ma'am," he said, "but I can't see my brother."

"Let's wait and see, shall we?" she said, but Jimmy didn't take his eyes from the ship.

"You don't want to be looking over there," said Paddy. "That's the ship we've left. We have to look for the ship that's coming to pick us up."

"Oh!" I said. "Is someone coming for us?"

"Those men in the radio room have been sending out signals ever since we first knew we had a problem," he said. "They're sending signals to anyone who can hear us. All we have to do is stay afloat until the help comes, and that won't be too hard, now, will it?"

But there were only stars and the other lifeboats bobbing on the sea. The women rowed steadily, the oars dipping and splashing.

Someone in the water was crying out to us and swimming towards our boat. I think he must have jumped from the ship, hoping that a lifeboat would take him on board. He reached us, gasping and wincing with cold, and his hands were turning blue-white with cold as he grabbed the side.

"Get off!" screamed someone as he tried

to pull himself into the boat. "You'll have us over! Somebody push him off!" But some of the women took pity on him and pulled him on board, where he lay huddled on the deck, his teeth chattering. More swimmers were in the water.

"We can't take them all on," said Paddy grimly. "If we overload the boat we'll all go under. The ship's going down and we need to be well out of her way before she does."

I covered my face with my hands and pretended not to know that we were rowing away from the men in the water, because it wasn't a thing I could bear. When we were a little further out I whispered to Paddy, though I could hardly speak for cold.

"Where are we going?" I asked.

"We're getting well out of the ship's way," he said. "She's going to go down and there'll be a great stirring up of the water when she does."

"But how can we tell where we are, and where we're going?" asked Jimmy.

Paddy smiled gently. "Look and I'll show you!" he said. "Do you see the stars? That's our map, so it is!"

He was calm and kind, pointing out the stars as he steered the boat further away from the *Titanic*. I suppose he was trying to distract us from the ship, but we could still hear people crying out and the distant sound of ragtime. I don't know how long it was before the music stopped.

But at last it did stop, and instead of the ragtime came music so sweet and sad that my throat grew thick and tight with crying, and scalding hot tears ran down my cold, cold face. *Titanic's* lights were still on, and she looked low in the water as if she was dying.

"Keep rowing, ladies," said Paddy. They did, though one of the women nearly lost an oar when her hands were too cold to grip. I was trying to keep warm by imagining a fire when Jimmy said,

"Oh, look!"

The ship wasn't straight any longer. Her line of lights sloped, the stern was higher than the bow. On deck, people were running to the stern as she tilted, and then –

– I still hate to think of it –

– and then her lights went out, and everything was dark. There was rumbling, roaring and a crash and I knew that everything was sliding down to the bow, all the furniture, the china and glass, the boxes, even the lovely staircase, all tumbling and smashing helplessly down so that the ship tilted even more. The stern rose until it stood up, pointing into the sky like a gravestone, then the great *Titanic* slid down to the bottom of the ocean and the icy water closed over her.

Some of the women on the boat covered their faces. Jimmy gazed and gazed at where the ship had gone down, his eyes wide as if he couldn't believe it. Paddy put a hand on his shoulder but I don't know if Jimmy even noticed. And the worst was the screaming, loud, terrible screaming of the people in the water, on and on – at first I covered my ears, then I covered Edwin's ears instead. Paddy made the sign of the cross.

"It'll all be over soon, sweetheart," he said. "Brave girl. Keep your eyes on the North Star now." He raised his voice. "We need to keep the lifeboats close together, so. Has anyone got a light, to signal to the other boats?"

A woman wearing her husband's jacket

found a box of matches in the pocket, and somebody else had a bit of paper. They lit the paper, held it up to show where we were, then dropped it in the sea where it disappeared with a hiss. I held Edwin as tightly as I could.

That night seemed to last for ever and ever. From time to time I began to fall asleep, but the sounds of crying and the creaking oars woke me, and every time I woke it was still dark. How long could a night last?

I tried to sing to Edwin − *Daisy, Daisy, give me your answer do...* − as the band had played for me, but my lips were too cold to make the words. It seemed to have been another world, or another life, when the band played to me in that busy, comfortable lounge. Rowers' hands, numb with cold, slipped from the oars. My ears, toes and fingers stung. Water had slopped into the bottom of the boat, and my feet were soaked and sore with cold. The man we'd picked up from the water wasn't moving. I felt that if I cried, the tears would freeze on my face.

I must have been falling asleep. In a dream I was sitting by the fire in Jimmy's room, but I was still cold. Edwin woke me.

"I'm hungry," he said, and I knew he was remembering the lovely hot food on the *Titanic*.

"Let's see what we can do," said Paddy. There was a box of plain biscuits under a seat and some flasks of water. It wouldn't have gone far around all of us, but most of the adults didn't want anything.

"Look, Daisy!" said Freddie suddenly, and pointed. A white flash rose into the sky.

"A rocket!" said Paddy. "There's a ship somewhere. Courage, now! Somebody light a paper!"

We couldn't see the ship, but we kept lighting papers so we could see and be seen. In one of those glows of light I saw Ma's white, tired face above the oar.

"Hold Edwin, will you?" I asked Jimmy. I picked my way carefully to her side and put my hands on the oar.

"Thank goodness for that," she said, and in spite of everything she smiled. "My hands were so cold I thought I'd drop it, then where would we be?"

Rowing helped to take my mind off the cold. Paddy lit a cigarette and I watched that point of orange light and heard him telling the boys about the stars. At last I dropped off to sleep against Ma, and when I woke the sky wasn't quite so dark. Morning would come, and we were still alive. Paddy was staring at something in the distance, and I followed his gaze.

"A ship!" I cried. "Ma, a ship!"

It really was! As dawn drew near, that big strong ship, the *Carpathia*, was coming to rescue us, and she was the most beautiful sight in the world.

# CHAPTER NINE

Doors were opened onto one of the decks, and they looked like a way into heaven. We still had a long wait – there were so many lifeboats, and so many people in them. Edwin was crying, Freddie looked about to cry, and the smallest thing would have set me off, too. The *Carpathia* crew lowered ladders down the side of the ship, but not all the passengers went up that way. They used big sacks as well, the mail sacks that they use for letters. When it was my turn, my hands were too numb to grip the ladder, so they swung a mail sack over the side for Edwin and me and hauled us up to the safety of the deck. But my legs were so cramped that they wouldn't hold me up and I fell to the deck with Edwin in my arms. Two of the crewmen helped me to stand up, and somebody else wrapped blankets round the boys.

"She's had enough," said one of the crewmen. I didn't realize that he meant me until he carried me to a lounge and set me down on a couch. We sat sipping hot coffee but I had to help Freddie with his because his hands were shaking so much.

Nobody spoke – I mean, the people from *Carpathia* did, but not us from *Titanic*. We had watched people die and heard them cry out. We'd lost everything. What was there to say?

The *Carpathia* passengers knew what had happened and wanted to help, and one of them came to talk to Ma. She was lovely.

She and her husband let us use her stateroom and lent clothes to Ma and me, because everything we had on was wet. My brothers were wrapped up in blankets while their clothes dried, and Jimmy was given a sweater that reached almost to his knees. Out of the boys' pockets came Freddie's best toy soldier and Edwin's rabbit. They still had their black-and-gold ribbons with '*Titanic*' embroidered on them, the ribbons we had bought so they'd always remember this journey!

"Put those away, Daisy," said Ma. "I don't want to see them."

"I'm going on deck," announced Jimmy. "I need to find my brother."

"What's your brother's name, honey?" asked the woman.

"Augus... Gus Gifford," he said.

"I'll ask the stewards to look out for him," she told him. "You get warm and rest."

Now that the boys were warming up, they were rubbing their eyes and yawning. Edwin had his rabbit and Freddie had his soldier, and they curled up with their treasures in their hands. After a while, Edwin suddenly asked,

"Where's the nice man?"

"What nice man, lamb?" I asked.

"The man on the ladder," he said.

"I don't know, lamb," I said.

Ma just sat, saying nothing, and Jimmy

insisted on going on deck. Stiffly and slowly, like an old lady, Ma got up, helped me on to the bed and pulled the quilt over me.

"You did well," she said. "Now get warm and rest."

I put my arms round Edwin and felt the warmth seep through me. Then I knew nothing at all until the sound of crying woke me.

It was Jimmy. Gus was not on the *Carpathia*. The two little children who had been playing in the cabin were safe with their mother, and they had seen him carrying a child up a ladder. That was the last anyone saw of him until his body was found in the water. I didn't know what to say to Jimmy.

# CHAPTER TEN

On the evening of Thursday 18 April, we were ready to dock at New York. The *Titanic* survivors were all on deck, ready to leave, but none of us had any luggage. We only had each other.

We hadn't expected such a crowd. It wasn't just the families coming to meet passengers off the ship – the *Titanic* story was in all the newspapers, and there seemed to be big flashing cameras everywhere so that I had to squint and shield my eyes.

"Will Pa still be here to meet us?" asked Freddie, because we were a day late.

"Should be," said Ma. "I hope he can find us in all this."

I scanned the crowds, all those people, all in black. I couldn't see Pa, but I knew he'd be there. Jimmy was still with us as if we'd adopted him. Gus had left him in Ma's care, and she took that very seriously.

"My parents will be here," he said. "Mrs Hooper, I guess I'll have to tell them about Gus."

"Would you like me to do that?" she said, and he nodded. He'd been such fun on the ship. Now he was subdued and quiet and could hardly say Gus's name without his eyes filling. The gangway was lowered, and the first-class passengers were to go before the rest of us.

"Gifford?" called a steward. "Is Jimmy Gifford here? Your parents are waiting in the passenger office."

"We're together," said Ma, so we trailed along behind her and Jimmy, Edwin holding tight to my hand. A tall, beautiful woman with her eyes red and small from crying and a haggard look as if she hadn't slept for days, threw her arms round Jimmy and then looked over his head to talk to Ma, then a clear, familiar voice, the best voice in the world, shouted, "Daisy! Boys! Daisy, over here!"

There was my Pa, my good, strong Pa, and for that moment he was all I wanted. Soon he was hugging me and the boys, and somehow after that first hug I believed that life might be good again. We were together, we had a home. Presently Ma appeared without Jimmy.

"Where's your luggage?" asked Pa, and Ma shook her head.

"No matter," he said. "You're here. That's all that matters."

Walking away with my hand in Pa's hand, I saw Jimmy walking away with his parents and I knew that, somehow, he would learn to live without Gus. He waved, and then the whole family got into an enormous black car.

"Where's Jimmy going?" asked Freddie.

"Home," I said. "He lives here in New York."

"Are we going to Silverpenny?" asked Edwin happily.

"Pennsylvania," I said. "Yes. And it'll be good."

We had survived the *Titanic*, but I would always remember the ones who didn't. My life had been saved, and I had to make the most of every moment of it. I owed it to Gus Gifford and all the passengers – more than a thousand of them – who never reached New York.

# EPILOGUE

*Titanic* and her sister ship, *Olympic*, were designed by the White Star Line to be the biggest and most luxurious liners ever built. They were to be mail ships, carrying post, but would be most famous for taking passengers across the Atlantic. As well as the wealthy first-class customers in superb staterooms, they would take poor immigrants travelling in steerage to make a better life in America. Because of her double hull with its separate compartments, *Titanic* was believed to be unsinkable.

On her first (or 'maiden') voyage, *Titanic* left Southampton on 10 April 1912, stopping twice to pick up passengers. For four days she was a wonderful floating hotel. Then, at twenty minutes to midnight on 14 April, she hit an iceberg which tore a hole in the hull, and in less than three hours she was at the bottom of the sea. She still lies there now, a hundred years later. Fish swim in and out of the portholes, and limpets cling to the rails.

Two thousand and seven people were on board *Titanic*. More than one thousand five hundred drowned when she went down, including most of the crew.

The *Titanic* story is full of 'if only' moments. At the last minute, the captain was changed. Captain Edward Smith was the most senior captain on the White Star Line and was about to retire. The directors of the White Star Line thought that no other captain was good enough for *Titanic's* maiden voyage. It may be that he was too eager to make a fast crossing.

There were other last-minute crew changes, too, and in the confusion an officer left the ship still carrying the key to the box with the binoculars in it. There was no other key on board. With binoculars, do you think the crew might have seen the iceberg in time?

Other ships in the area warned *Titanic* of icebergs, but Captain Smith carried on at a fast pace. Was he trying to make the maiden voyage impressively fast? Also, radio contact on board ship was quite a new and exciting thing. The officers were busy making calls to New York for the first-class passengers, and didn't always pay attention to other ships.

There were sixteen wooden lifeboats and four collapsible ones. Between them there was room for one thousand, one hundred and seventy-eight passengers, not enough for all the passengers and crew. But at the time, this was not against the law!

There are hundreds of stories of heroism from the sinking of the *Titanic*. Perhaps the most moving is the story of the band, who stayed in their places and kept playing until they went down with the ship, making no attempt to save their own lives. The youngest survivor was two-month-old baby Milvina Dean, who lived to be ninety-seven.

This story and the characters are fictional, but they are based on historical facts. There really was a crewman called Paddy who helped to keep people calm in the boats, and who showed one of the girls how to navigate by the stars. And there really were children who played in *Titanic's* empty cabins.

Also available...

I Was There...

Step back into
Roman Britain

BOUDICA'S ARMY

*Queen Boudica was leading the great spreading rabble. I didn't know there were so many people in the world. So many horses. So many swords.*

I Was There...

Step back into the fight for York

VIKING INVASION

*My words were drowned as suddenly the world seemed to be split apart by a huge yell that roared in the air. The Viking war-cry!*

I Was There...

Step back into the Battle of Hastings

1066

CLANG! CLANG! CLANG!

*The sounds of sword blades crashing against sword blades, and axes smashing on wooden shields echoed from the battlefield.*

# I Was There...

Step back into the life of a medieval prince

## RICHARD III

*We are going to battle! But will I be brave enough to fight like a Prince of the House of York!*

# I Was There...

Step back into
the life of
a young actor

## SHAKESPEARE'S GLOBE

*I don't want to be a farmhand or a butcher.
I want to be a player on the stage at the
Globe playhouse in London!*

# I Was There...

Step back into
Victorian England

## ROYAL NURSEMAID

*"I've just heard something amazing."* Jane
sounded so excited it made my fingers tingle.
*"Queen Victoria is expecting another baby!"*

I Was There...

Step back into the trenches of the First World War

**ALONE IN THE TRENCHES**

"Well, bless my soul. What 'ave we 'ere then?" I could make out the shapes of two men. One in a soldier's uniform...

# I Was There...

Step back into Egypt's Valley of the Kings

## TUTANKHAMUN'S TOMB

*Carter ran his hand over the stone. No one moved. No one spoke. Everyone's eyes were fixed on him. I held my breath. Was it the step? Or wasn't it?*

I Was There...

Step back into Second World War Britain

ESCAPE FROM THE BLITZ

*It was all pretty terrifying if I really let myself think about it — being sent off to live with strangers, bombs being dropped...*

You'll be able to imagine
you were really there!